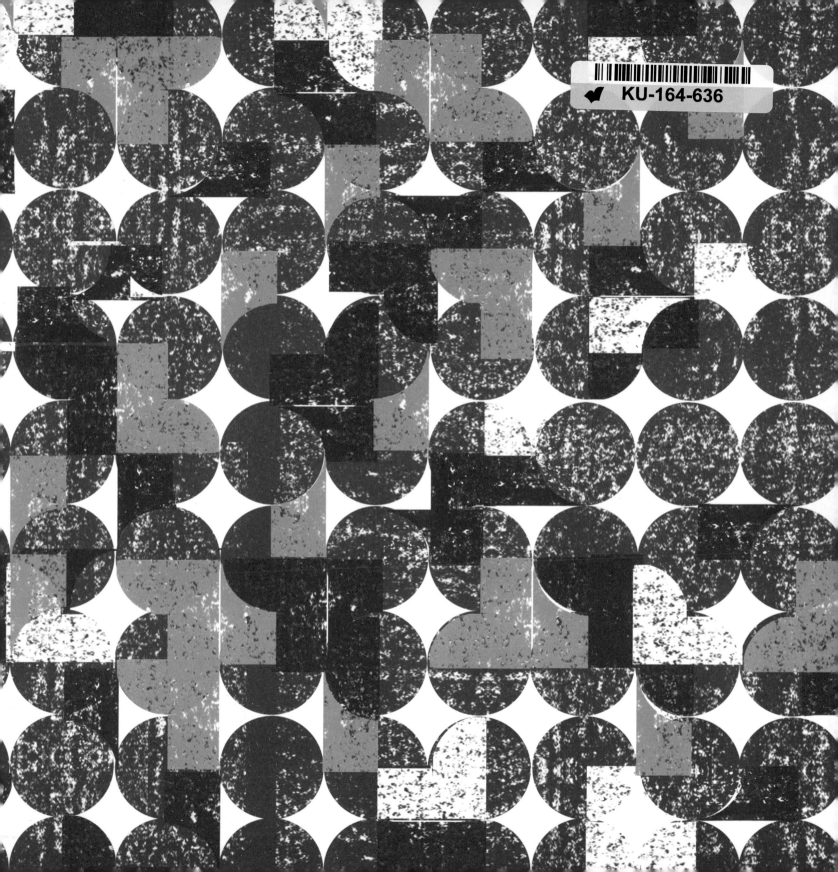

First published 2016 by order of the Tate Trustees
by Tate Publishing, a division of Tate Enterprises Ltd,
Millbank, London SW1P 4RG
www.tate.org.uk/publishing

A catalogue record for this book is available from the British Library
ISBN 978 1 84976 349 3

Distributed in the United States and Canada by ABRAMS, New York

Library of Congress Control Number applied for

Designed by The Studio of Williamson Curran
Colour reproduction by C&C Offset Printing Co. Ltd
Printed and bound by C&C Offset Printing Co. Ltd

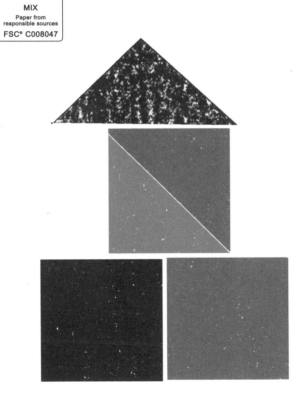

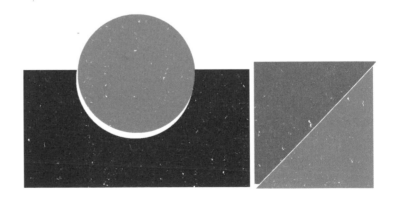

Did you ever see?

Joanna Walsh

Tate Publishing

Did you ever look ...

... down
from a high window
or from a plane
and see the city streets,
neat lines and squares?

Or lie down on the ground and look
up at the sky
and wonder how high
the clouds might be?

What's the tallest thing that you can see?

The highest tree?
A crane?
A high-rise tower?
Are you sure?
And would it be taller than
a dinosaur?

And what's the smallest thing?

A speck of dirt?
An ant's left foot?

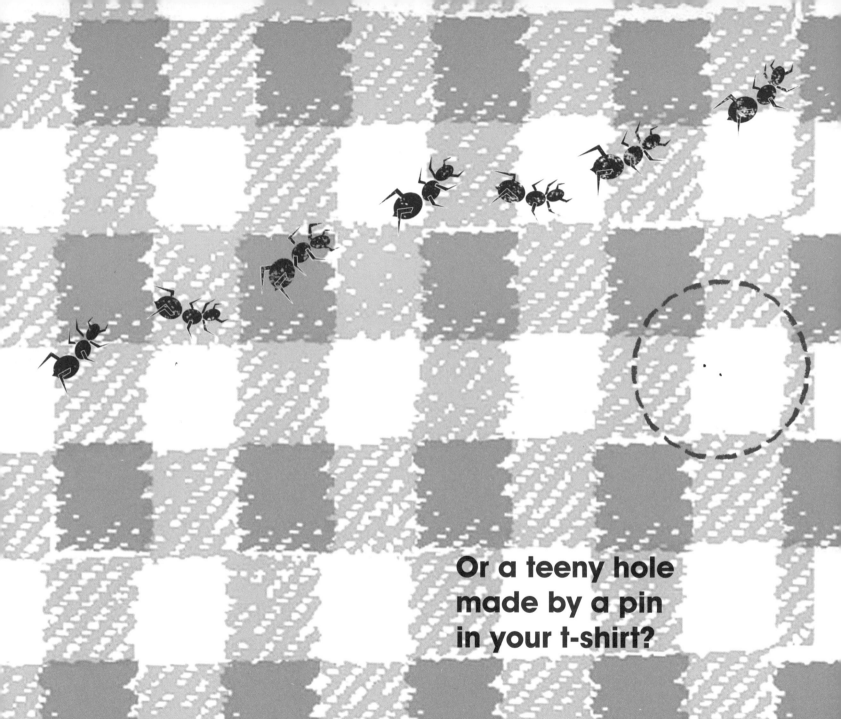

**Or a teeny hole
made by a pin
in your t-shirt?**

But did you ever see anything even smaller?

A tiny microbe under a shiny microscope?

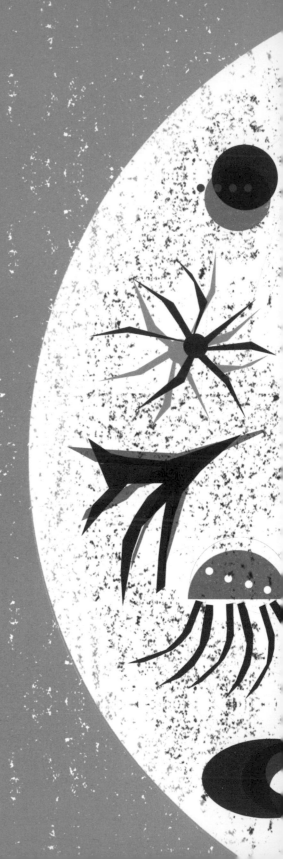

If you've already seen that, wouldn't you like to see what's inside a seed?

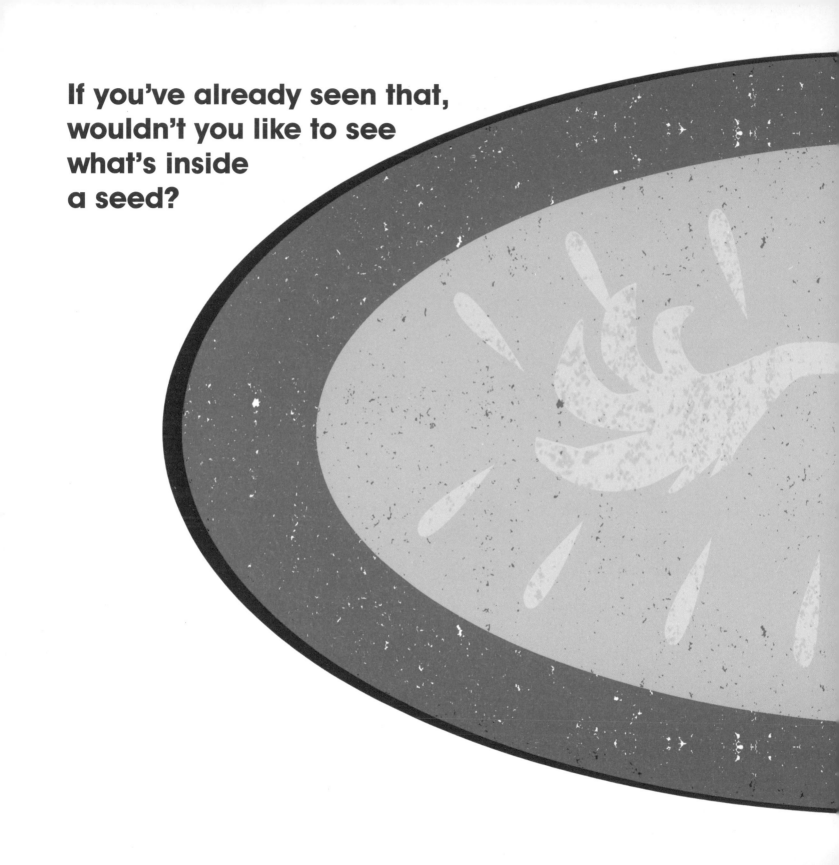

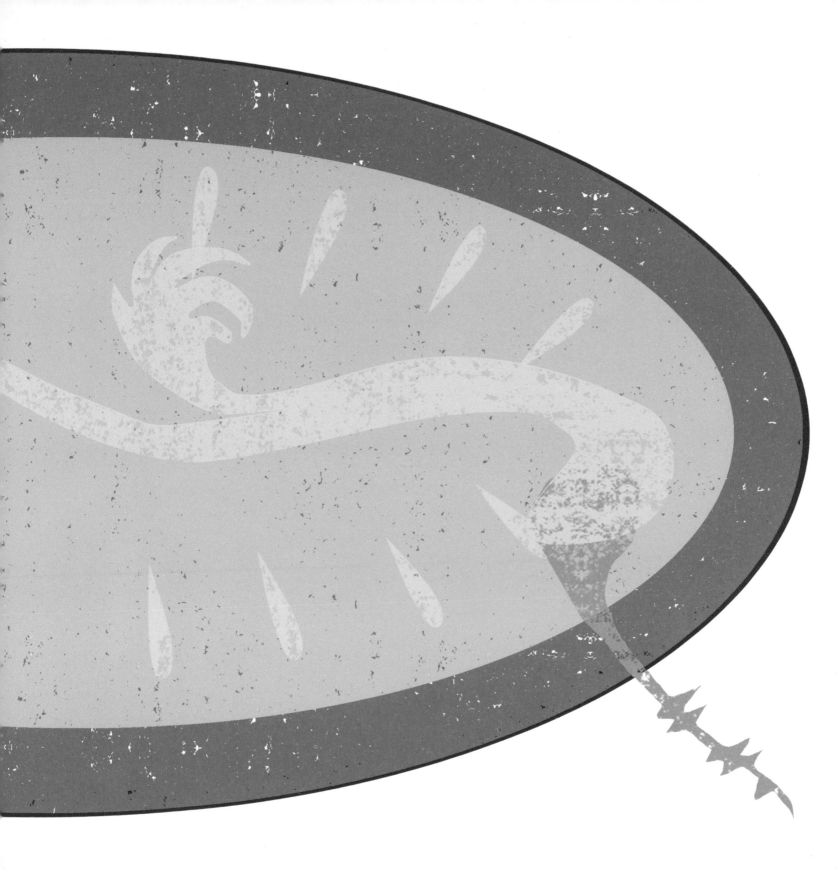

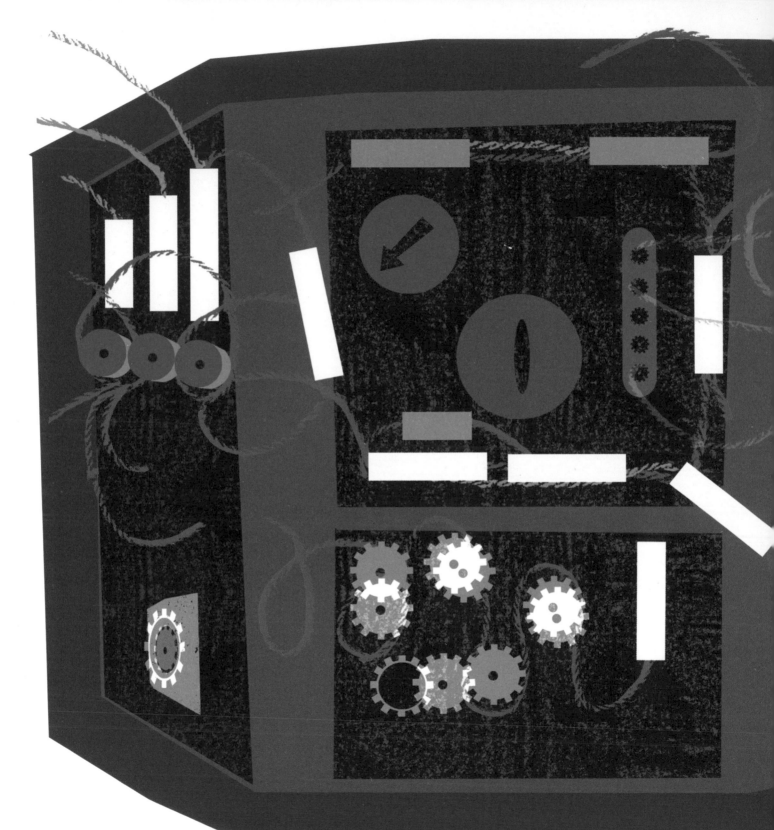

An old TV?
Or ...

... the filling from
the middle of a pillow?

In a mirror
did you ever
see such a sight?

What's right is wrong,
what's left is right.

Have you ever sped past
in such a hurry

that everything you passed
was soft and blurry?

**And did you ever squeeze your eyes so tight
that you see lots and lots
of dots of light?**

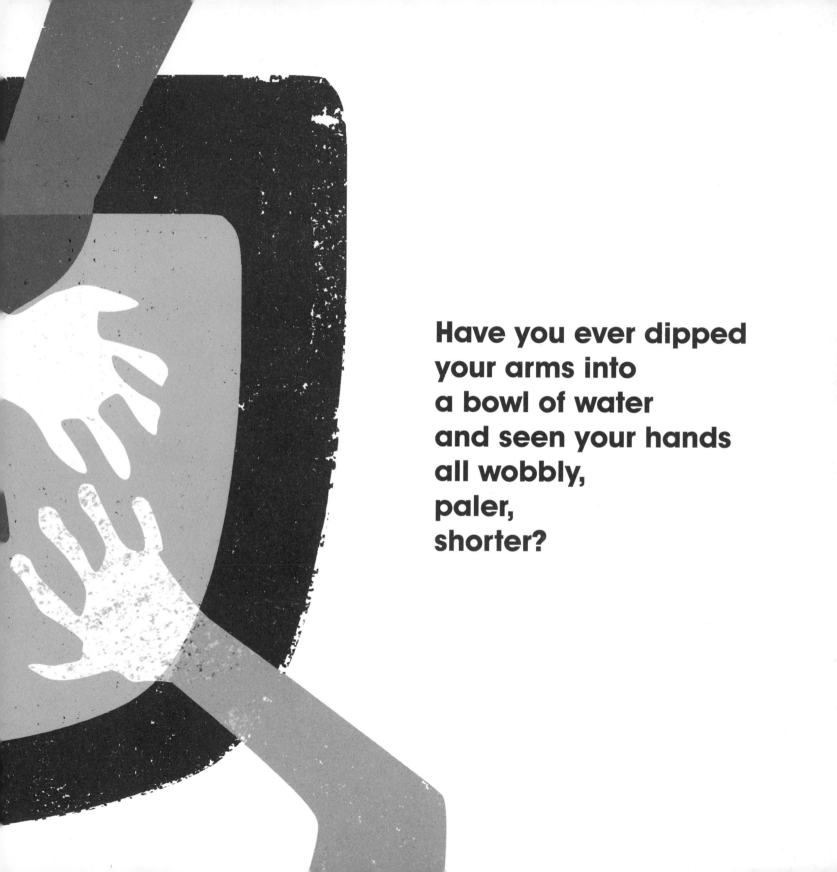

**Have you ever dipped
your arms into
a bowl of water
and seen your hands
all wobbly,
paler,
shorter?**

Have you ever seen
anything so far as
– light years away –
the farthest star?

**But the best thing of all to see
is far off, getting nearer**

**a friend smiling,
walking towards you ...**

... clearer and clearer.